Traction Man

meets

Turbodog

MINI GREY

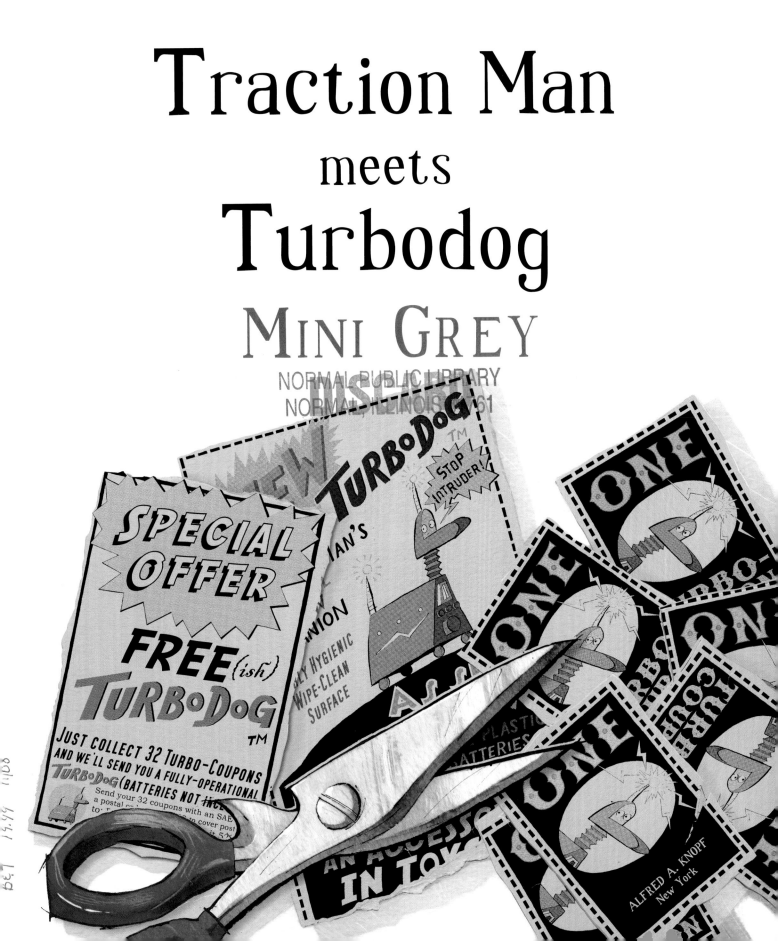

SPECIAL OFFER

FREE *(ish)*
TURBODOG ™

JUST COLLECT 32 Turbo-Coupons
AND WE'LL SEND YOU A FULLY-OPERATIONAL
TURBODOG (BATTERIES NOT INC...

Send your 32 coupons with an SAE...
a postal ...
to...
on cover post...
it 5...

TURBODOG ™

STOP INTRUDER!

...LY HYGIENIC
WIPE-CLEAN
SURFACE

...PLASTIC
...BATTERIES

AN ACCESS...
IN TO...

ONE

ALFRED A. KNOPF
New York

...and PLEASE stay out of the mud today.

Traction Man is here!
(And his faithful pet Scrubbing Brush too!)

Traction Man and Scrubbing Brush
are on the Northwest Slope
of Mt. Compost Heap.

Traction Man is
wearing his Rubber
Rescue Harness,
Glacier Boots
and lots of rope.

LONG WAY UP
WE ARE

Scrubbing Brush
is carrying LUNCH.

This Ancient Potato
is guiding them to the top.

The only way back is through the swampy marshes of the Pond.

They can cross by Boot.

Traction Man and Scrubbing Brush are drying off in front of the heater.

Traction Man is wearing a knotted spotted hanky.

Scrubbing Brush is encrusted with dried-on dirt.

Everyone is warm and sleepy.

Traction Man and Turbodog are crossing the wastes of the Sandpit.

Somewhere under the shifting sands are the ruins of the Handbag.

Maybe that's a corner of it there. The Handbag Dwellers are very shy.

Traction Man and Turbodog are watching Turbodog's greatest adventures on TV.

STOP INTRUDER!

Turbodog thinks it is just getting to the good bit.
This is what Turbodog likes to do BEST.

INSERT BATTERY HERE

Scrubbing Brush!
I must find my brave pet!
Where can Scrubbing Brush be?

Never run out of hope!
Never give up!
Scrubbing Brush
will be **somewhere**.

Green Nun
General Purpose Wine

Château
Chat

But Traction Man
has looked just
about everywhere.

Aaaaaarf

Did you hear that?

He wears his Airtight Astro-Suit
with Glass Head-Globe.
The atmosphere at the Bin's surface
may be deadly poisonous.

Traction Man takes
a bottle of
**SuperStrong
GERMO**
(with Ammonia).

No one has ever
returned alive from
the Bin before.

SUPER
STRONG
GERMO
with
AMMONIA

These Evil Creatures are gathered round a shivering bundle of potato peelings.

ssstay.

We will have you.

We likes you.

"I wonder . . ."

We wants you.

HOOPO

stain cake

"Scrubbing Brush, it's you!"

"Run and don't look round! Whatever you do, don't listen to the tormenting cries of the Bin-Things."
Come back.
We wants you.
We needs you.
"Phew! Good work, Scrubbing Brush."

Traction Man and Scrubbing Brush are going free diving in the Steaming Tropical Waters of the Tub. Turbodog has come too.

I WILL BE YOUR PET

Traction Man is wearing his Elasticized Micro-Suit, Shark Knife and Slimline Snorkel.

Turbodog is floating on the SS Sponge.

Scrubbing Brush is looking much cleaner.

There's a fizz and a flicker.

CLUNK

Oh dear.

Traction Man and Scrubbing Brush are
Surviving for the afternoon in the
shrubbery near the Pond.
Traction Man has his Magnetic Compass,
First-Aid Kit and Survival Vest.
They have constructed a shelter from
pillowcases and a bath mat.

The Dollies are looking after Turbodog.
He is very quiet now. (They had to
take out his rusty batteries.)

Scrubbing Brush is wearing a
Badge of Cleanness
and has been foraging for Supplies.
Traction Man is helping
Scrubbing Brush to stay clean.
And of course, they are both
Prepared for
Anything.

A Present for SCRUBBING BRUSH from Dad

melt
MAL

THIS IS A BORZOI BOOK PUBLISHED BY ALFRED A. KNOPF

Copyright © 2008 by Mini Grey

All rights reserved. Published in the United States by Alfred A. Knopf, an imprint of
Random House Children's Books, a division of Random House, Inc., New York.
Published in Great Britain in 2008 by Jonathan Cape, an imprint of Random House Children's Books.

Knopf, Borzoi Books, and the colophon are registered trademarks of Random House, Inc.

Visit us on the Web! www.randomhouse.com/kids

Educators and librarians, for a variety of teaching tools, visit us at www.randomhouse.com/teachers

Library of Congress Cataloging-in-Publication Data
Grey, Mini.
Traction Man meets Turbodog / by Mini Grey. — 1st American ed.
p. cm.
Summary: Traction Man, an action figure, teams up with the high-tech but not-so-bright Turbodog to rescue
Scrubbing Brush, his missing sidekick, from the terrible underworld of the bin.
ISBN 978-0-375-85583-2 (trade) — ISBN 978-0-375-95583-9 (lib. bdg.)
[1. Action figures (Toys)—Fiction. 2. Brooms and brushes—Fiction. 3. Toys—Fiction.
4. Lost and found possessions—Fiction.] I. Title.
PZ7.G873Trm 2008
[E]—dc22
2007041525

MANUFACTURED IN MALAYSIA
September 2008
10 9 8 7 6 5 4 3 2 1

First American Edition

THE MYSTERIOUS SHROOMS
WOULD LIKE TO THANK
STEVE COLE FOR HIS HELP
WITH THEIR TEAMWORK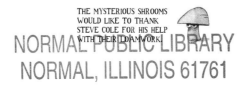